5 MINUTE Fairy Tales

bookoli

Published in 2020 by Bookoli,
12 Laura Place, Bath BA2 4BL.
Bookoli is an imprint of Curious Universe UK Ltd.
Copyright © 2020 Curious Universe UK Ltd.
www.curiousuniverse.co.uk

CONTENTS

Little Red Riding Hood

Once there was a girl called
Little Red Riding Hood who lived
on the edge of a deep, dark wood.

One day, her mother asked her
to take a basket of cakes to her
grandma's cottage in the forest.
"But make sure you stick to the
path," said her mother. "And watch
out for the Big, Bad Wolf!"

Little Red Riding Hood skipped along the path into the forest. Suddenly, out from the trees jumped the Big, Bad Wolf!

"Where are you going, my dear?" he growled.
"To my grandma's cottage," said Little Red Riding Hood. The wolf grinned.
"Why not pick her some lovely flowers?"

"What a good idea,"
said Little Red Riding Hood,
stepping off the path. But the
sly wolf had a plan. He would
get to Grandma's cottage first.
"Then I'll gobble them both up!"
he drooled. The wolf slunk away as
Little Red Riding Hood picked the flowers.

Maybe the wolf isn't so bad after all...

Tap-tap! went the wolf on the cottage door.
"Come in, dear," said Grandma,
thinking it was Little Red Riding Hood.

The Big, Bad Wolf leapt inside! He grabbed
Grandma and shoved her into a cupboard.
Then he quickly put on her nightdress and cap,
and climbed into her bed. Suddenly, there was
another tap-tap at the door.

"Hello," said Little Red Riding Hood, stepping inside.
But there was something strange about Grandma...

"Your ears are awfully big and furry!"

"All the better to hear you with," said the wolf sweetly.

"And what big, black eyes you have!"

"All the better to see you with," said the wolf, grinning.

Little Red Riding Hood suddenly felt afraid.
"Grandma, your teeth look very sharp..."

"All the better to **EAT** you with!" snarled the wolf,
leaping up. He chased Little Red Riding Hood around the room.
There was howling and screaming, and banging and crashing.

Luckily, a brave woodcutter was working nearby.
He heard the rumpus and burst into the cottage.
"Bully someone your own size!" he said to the wolf.

"AWOOOH!"

The cowardly wolf whimpered as the woodcutter
raised his sharp axe. The wolf dashed out of the door
and disappeared deep into the forest.

Grandma felt much better after a cake and a mug of hot chocolate. Little Red Riding Hood and the woodcutter did too.

After that, whenever she visited Grandma, Little Red Riding Hood always stayed on the path. She never stopped to pick flowers, and most importantly, she never saw the Big, Bad Wolf again.

"I have to go!"
cried Cinderella, as
she ran down the palace
steps. The fairy godmother's
spell was fading fast.

The coach sped away into the
night. All that was left was a single
glass slipper on the stair.

"I will marry the girl whose foot fits
this slipper," said the prince.

He had fallen in love with Cinderella.

The prince searched the entire kingdom, until at last he came to Cinderella's house. The two stepsisters pinched and pushed one another as they tried to grab the glass slipper.

"Me first!" they squealed.

But no matter how much they squashed and squeezed, the slipper would not fit. Then the prince spotted Cinderella scrubbing the floor

"You must try the slipper too,"
commanded the prince.

So Cinderella crept shyly into the room. Her ragged dress was dirty from cleaning the fireplace.

She lowered her foot into the delicate glass slipper. It was a perfect fit.

The prince married Cinderella and she became a real princess. Never again would she have to wear rags or cook and clean.

Cinderella forgave her wicked stepmother and stepsisters, but they were so jealous, they left the kingdom and never came back.

Cinderella and her prince lived happily ever after.

The Three Little Pigs

Once upon a time, three little pigs left home
to explore the big, wide world.

"Make sure that greedy wolf doesn't eat you,"
said their mother. The little pigs didn't want to be
wolf snacks, so each one decided to build a house.

The first little pig wanted to build his house from straw.

The second little pig chose to build his house from sticks.

The third little pig built his house from strong, red bricks. He was sure he would be safe from the greedy wolf in there!

21

Sure enough, the greedy wolf arrived at the house of straw.

"Little pig, little pig, let me come in!"

"Not by the hair on my chinny chin chin. I will not let you in!" grunted the first little pig. "Well, I'll huff and I'll puff and I'll blow your house in!" said the wolf.

Soon the house of straw was flattened.

22

Next, the wolf went to the house of sticks.
"Little pig, little pig, let me come in!"

"Not by the hair on my chinny chin chin. I will not let you in!" squealed the second little pig.

"I'll **huff** and I'll **puff** and I'll blow your house in!"

Soon the house of sticks was demolished.

Feeling very confident, the wolf came to the house of bricks.

"Little pig, little pig, let me come in!"

sang the wicked wolf.

"Not by the hair on my chinny chin chin.
I will NOT let you in!" oinked the third little pig.

The wolf huffed and he puffed. He puffed and he huffed...

But no matter how hard he blew, the house of bricks stood firm. The wolf was very angry.

"I'll get you piggies!" he snarled. He bounded onto the roof and jumped down the chimney.

Luckily the third, and cleverest, little pig had a plan.

And what a surprise that greedy wolf got!

He ran away, clutching his scorched bottom, and never came back. From then on, the three little pigs lived happily together in the house of bricks.

Rapunzel

Once upon a time there lived a girl called Rapunzel who had long, golden hair. But a wicked witch was jealous of Rapunzel's beauty. She stole her away and locked her in a tall tower. Each day, the witch called up to Rapunzel.

The girl would lower her hair and let the witch climb up.

Rapunzel, Rapunzel, let down your hair!

27

One day, a prince rode past and heard Rapunzel singing sweetly. He wanted to climb up to the beautiful girl, but how?

Suddenly, the prince heard the witch call out. How astonished he was to see her scramble up Rapunzel's hair!

The prince hid until the witch had gone, and then...

Rapunzel, Rapunzel, let down your hair!

Once again, Rapunzel's tresses tumbled down the side of the tower. But she got quite a surprise when instead of the warty witch, a handsome prince appeared at her window.

Rapunzel was delighted! The prince told her wonderful stories of the world beyond her tower. They agreed to meet secretly every day.

But one morning, the witch clambered clumsily up Rapunzel's hair. She heaved and tugged.

"**Ouch!** I wish you climbed gently like my prince," complained Rapunzel.

"**Prince?**" screeched the witch, furiously. She snatched a pair of scissors from her pocket. Then she grabbed Rapunzel's hair and with a **snip-snip, cut it off.**

"Rapunzel, Rapunzel let down your hair!"

called the prince from the bottom of the tower.

The sly witch lowered the cut hair out of the window. When the prince climbed up it wasn't Rapunzel who greeted him, but the grinning witch! Her black eyes glinted as she let go of the hair.

Goodbye, Prince!

Aaargh!

31

The prince plunged to the ground. He landed in a tangle of thorns that scratched his eyes so he could not see. The evil witch cackled.

"I will hide Rapunzel in the forest, and you will never find her!" she shrieked.

Rapunzel disappeared from the tower and the prince staggered blindly into the forest.

Rapunzel was banished by the witch's spell, but she did not forget her prince. She was determined to rescue him, so for days and nights Rapunzel searched the forest, singing her sad song.

Then one evening she heard her name being called.

"Rapunzel, Rapunzel..."

It was the prince! Rapunzel held him close and her tears trickled onto his face. Then, as if by magic, the prince's eyes were healed and he could see again.

"Come and explore the world with me," he said.

Rapunzel agreed, and she and the prince went far away. They never saw the evil witch again and lived happily ever after.

Snow White

Once there lived a beautiful yet wicked queen. She was jealous of her pretty, young stepdaughter, Snow White. One day, the queen asked her magic mirror a question.

The mirror was bound to tell the truth and replied,
"Snow White is the fairest."

The queen flew into a rage. How dare Snow White be more beautiful than her! The queen summoned her huntsman.

"Take Snow White to the forest and kill her," she hissed.

So the huntsman took Snow White into the forest. But he could not kill her. She was too innocent and kind.

Run away, Snow White!

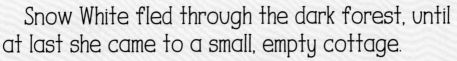

Snow White fled through the dark forest, until at last she came to a small, empty cottage.

Inside, a table was laid with seven places. And by the fire there were seven little beds. Snow White yawned. She was tired from all that running...

That evening, seven dwarfs returned home. What a surprise it was to find Snow White asleep in their cottage! She awoke and told them all about the wicked queen.

"You will be safe here with us," they said.

So Snow White stayed with the seven kind dwarfs. For a while she was very happy.

At the palace, the wicked queen looked in her magic mirror. "Mirror, mirror on the wall, who is the fairest of them all?" "Snow White is still the fairest," replied the mirror.

Snow White was alive!

The queen was furious, so she came up with an evil plan. She dipped an apple in poison, then she dressed up as an old woman.

In the forest, Snow White heard a knock on the door. Outside was a little old woman selling apples.

"Try this juicy red one, my dear,"
she said, smiling.

Snow White couldn't resist. She bit the shiny red apple, then she fell to the floor and lay as still as death.

How those dwarfs cried when they found their dear Snow White! They carried her into the forest in a glass coffin.

As they laid her down, a prince rode by. He fell in love with the beautiful girl at first sight.

She looks like she is just sleeping.

The prince kissed Snow White gently.

Then something amazing happened...

Snow White woke up, as if a spell was broken!

The dwarfs danced and cheered happily.

Snow White fell in love with the prince. They were soon married and lived happily ever after. Never again did the wicked queen trouble Snow White.

Jack and the Beanstalk

Jack and his mother lived in an old, crooked house on the hill. They were very poor, so one day Jack sold their only cow for some magic beans. His mother was cross.

"What use are some strange beans?"

But the enchanted beans sprouted into a gigantic beanstalk. It grew and grew, stretching up into the sky.

I'm going to climb the beanstalk!

At the top of the beanstalk, Jack saw
a huge castle in the clouds. He crept inside.
On the kitchen table was a big bag of gold coins.

Suddenly ... **thump, thump!** The ground
shook as a smelly, hairy giant appeared.

"Fee-fi-fo-fum,

I smell the blood of an Englishman.
Be he alive, or be he dead ..."

I'll grind his bones
to make my bread!

The greedy giant sat and gobbled up his dinner. Soon he fell fast asleep, so Jack took the bag of coins. He ran back to the beanstalk and climbed down.

That giant has awful table manners!

For a while, Jack and his mother were rich. But soon the gold coins ran out. So it wasn't long before Jack climbed back up the beanstalk.

Back in the castle, Jack was amazed to find a hen that laid golden eggs.

**"Fee-fi-fo-fum,
I smell the blood
of an Englishman,"**

grumbled the giant.
Just as before, he gobbled up his dinner and fell asleep. So Jack grabbed the hen and hurried back down the beanstalk.

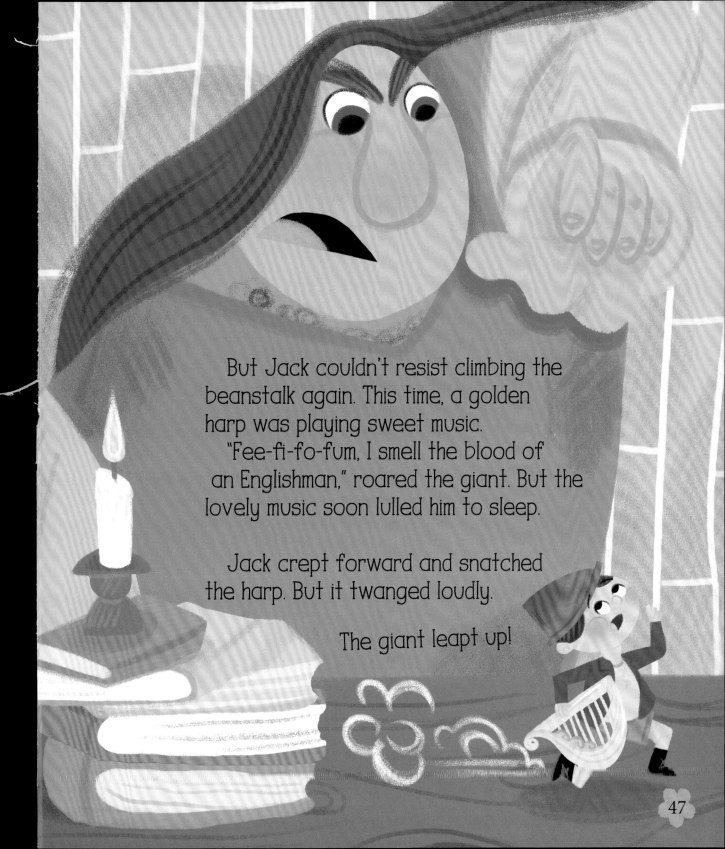

But Jack couldn't resist climbing the beanstalk again. This time, a golden harp was playing sweet music.

"Fee-fi-fo-fum, I smell the blood of an Englishman," roared the giant. But the lovely music soon lulled him to sleep.

Jack crept forward and snatched the harp. But it twanged loudly.

The giant leapt up!

Jack raced off down the beanstalk with the giant thundering behind him.

"Mother, fetch the axe!" Jack cried.

Chop-chop-chop

went Jack, as fast as he could. With a ripping and tearing, the beanstalk crashed to the ground.

That was the end of the hairy, smelly giant. And Jack and his mother were rich for the rest of their days.